For Mark: my explorer, my pioneer, my trailblazer

Imagination will often carry us to worlds that never were, but without it we go nowhere. —Carl Sagan

## About This Book

The illustrations for this book were done in pencil, India ink, gouache, and watercolor, and then collaged in Photoshop. The display type on the maps and in the speech bubbles was hand-lettered by the author. This book was edited by Mary-Kate Gaudet and designed by Jen Keenan. The production was supervised by Virginia Lawther, and the production editor was Jen Graham. The text was set in Bulletin Typewriter.

Copyright © 2018 by Deborah Marcero • Cover illustration copyright © 2018 by Deborah Marcero • Cover design by Jen Keenan • Cover copyright © 2018 by Hachette Book Group, Inc. • Hachette Book Group supports the right to free expression and the value of copyright. The purpose of copyright is to encourage writers and artists to produce the creative works that enrich our culture. • The scanning, uploading, and distribution of this book without permission is a theft of the author's intellectual property. If you would like permission to use material from the book (other than for review purposes), please contact permissions@hbgusa.com. Thank you for your support of the author's rights. • Little, Brown and Company • Hachette Book Group • 1290 Avenue of the Americas, New York, NY 10104 • Visit us at LBYR.com • First Edition: October 2018 • Little, Brown and Company is a division of Hachette Book Group, Inc. The Little, Brown name and logo are trademarks of Hachette Book Group, Inc. • The publisher is not responsible for websites (or their content) that are not owned by the publisher. • Library of Congress Cataloging-in-Publication Data • Names: Marcero, Deborah, author. • Title: My heart is a compass / by Deborah Marcero. • Description: First edition. | New York ; Boston : Little, Brown and Company, 2018. • Summary: "Rose wants to bring something truly unique for show-and-tell, so she creates maps to explore her imagination in search of something no one has ever seen before." —Provided by publisher. • Identifiers: LCCN 2017027421| ISBN 9780316561761 (hardcover) | ISBN 9780316561778 (ebook) | ISBN 9780316561785 (ebook) | ISBN 9780316561792 (ebook) • Subjects: | CYAC: Imagination—Fiction. | Cartography—Fiction. | Voyages and travels—Fiction. | Show-and-tell presentations—Fiction. • Classification: LCC PZ7.1.M3699 Com 2018 | DDC [E]—dc23 • LC record available at https://lccn.loc.gov/2017027421 • ISBNs: 978-0-316-56176-1 (hardcover), 978-0-316-56177-8 (ebook), 978-0-316-56178-5 (ebook), 978-0-316-56179-2 (ebook) • Printed in China • 1010 • 10 9 8 7 6 5 4 3 2 1

# My Heart Is a Compass

## Deborah Marcero

LITTLE, BROWN AND COMPANY
NEW YORK  BOSTON

Rose longed to be an explorer,
a pioneer, a trailblazer.

Her heart was set on discovering
something that had never been found ...

WAY TO M.T.
EVERST & C

... to bring to show-and-tell.

She had one problem:

She didn't know what it was or where to find it.

It could have been anything.

Something exotic?

Something magical?

Did it even exist?

Where could she find such a thing?

For that, she needed a map. Not an atlas or a globe.

To find the secret coordinates, she would
have to draw her own map.

As she sketched and scaled, Rose's hand quivered.
Her lines wiggled and shimmied off the page.

Her imagination became a blueprint, with her heart a compass.

She scooted off....

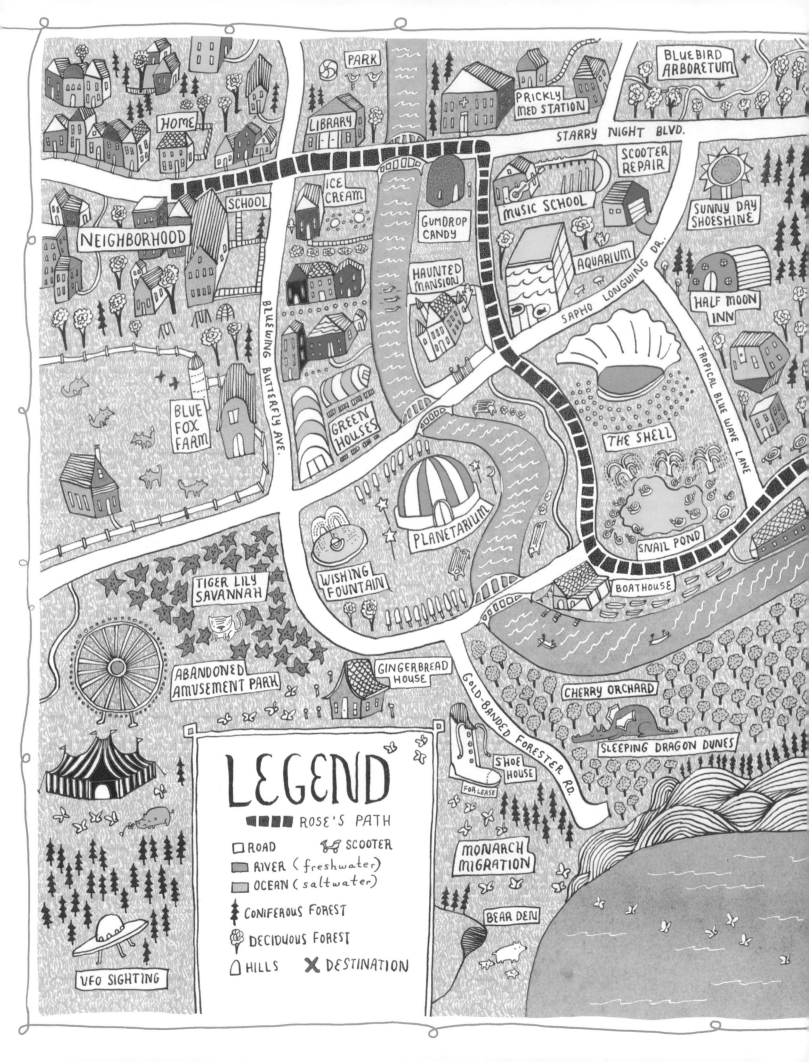

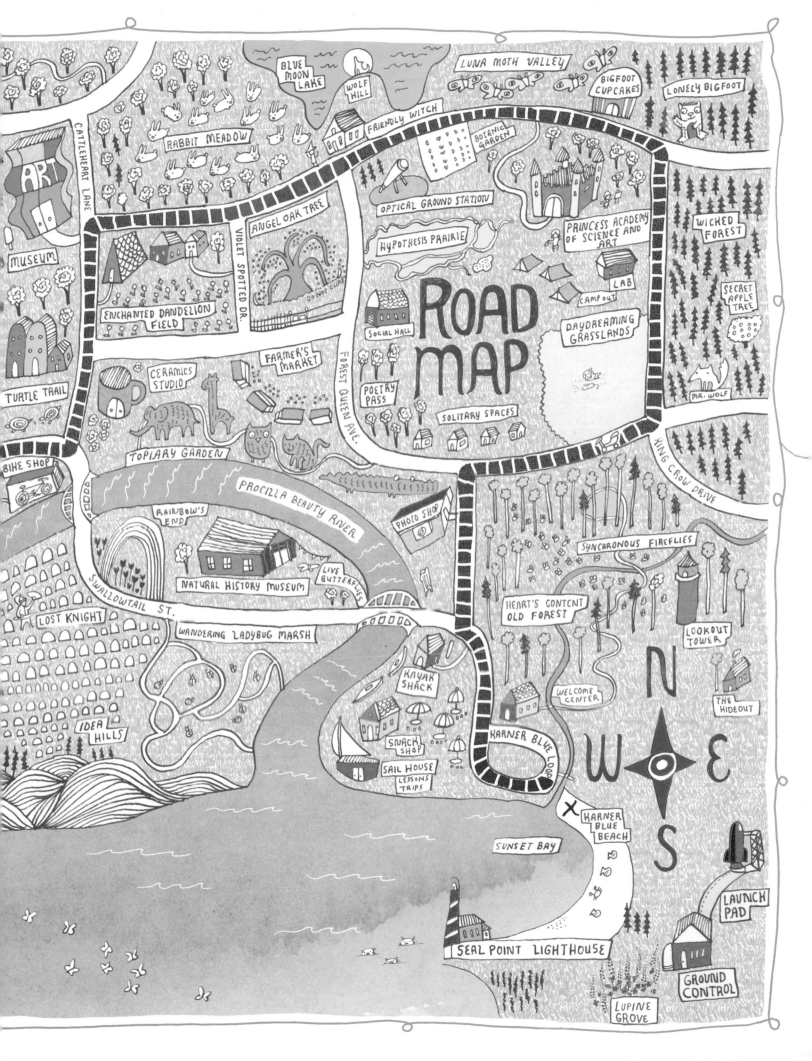

At the beach, Rose saw plenty of sea stars, shells, and gulls.
But there was no treasure to be found.

So Rose charted the sky and launched into the cosmos.

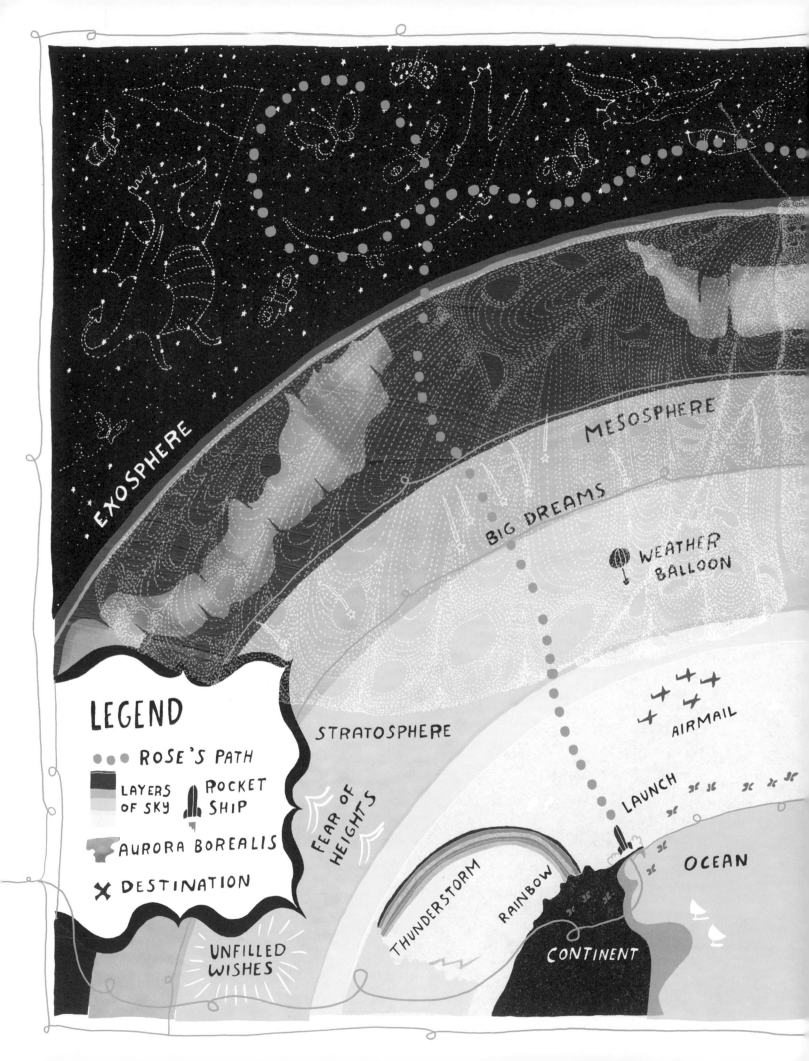

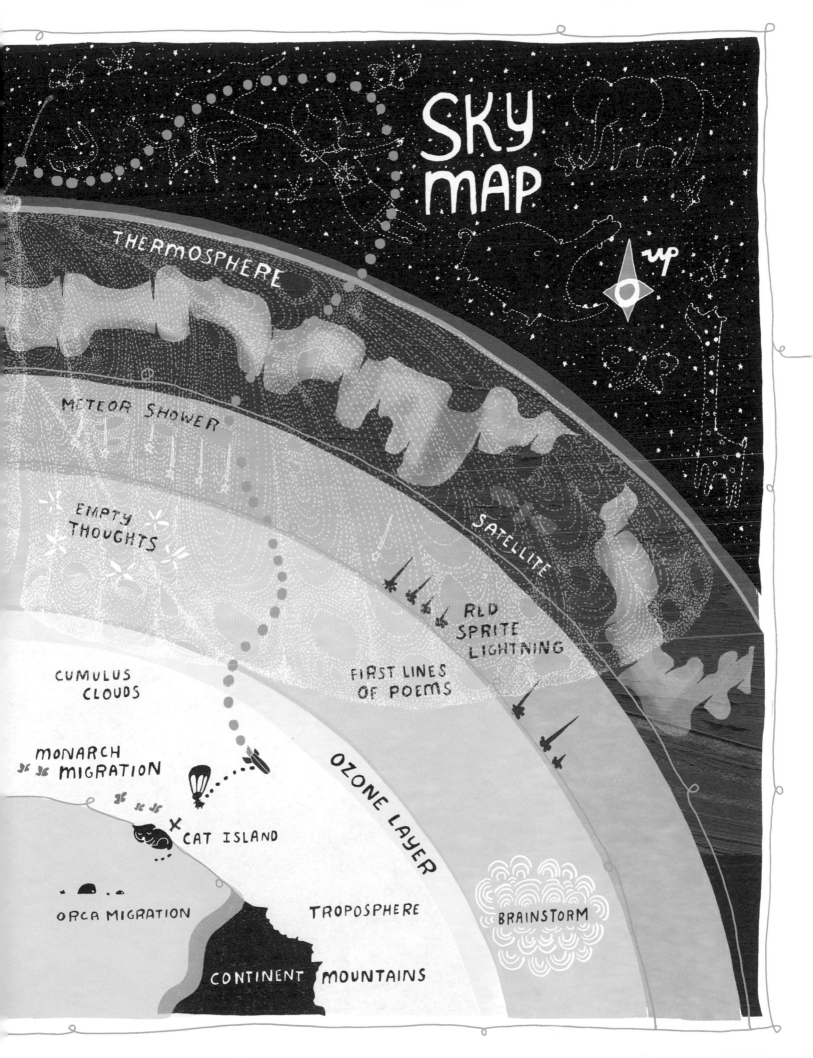

Although the atmosphere was full of adventure, shooting stars, and billowing northern lights, Rose parachuted to an island, still empty-handed.

So she mapped the ocean and set sail.

Pirate
Territory

Mermaid
Island

Ocean
Map

(topographical)

Owl
Enclave

Puff
Volcano

Reaching
Strait

Pod of
Playful
Dolphins

Sleeping
Dragon
Sea

Swallowtail
Archipelago

Secret
Submarine

Shark
Frenzy

Hippo's
Mouth
Bay

Thriving
Coral
Reef

Gentle Giant
Squid

N

Rose found harbor in a city where skyscrapers mirrored every cloud and rainbow, but there was no rare jewel to behold.

So she plotted train tracks into the mountains...

Search Rose's Maps

Elephant
Inlet

Last Stop

Owl
Circle

Cat Ear
Ridge

D.

Lake in the
Clouds

C.

B.

Secret
Lair

Blue Dragon Smoky
Mountains

A.

22

Starry Night
Forest

10mi

Terms

© Rose's Maps

...where she stepped off at the very last stop.

As the low sun painted the end of another day,
Rose knew she must return home with nothing in her pockets.

Nothing to show. Nothing to tell.

She found herself in the same place she began.

The next day in class, when Rose's turn came, her stomach sank.
And then she shared her story of searching—far and wide,
high and low—and returning empty-handed.

The class was silent.

Rose looked around the room and finally saw it too. She had found something no one had ever seen or heard before.

It was more than the world.
It was EVERYTHING she imagined.

She felt like

an explorer,

a pioneer,

a trailblazer.

And everyone who had the chance
to hear Rose's tale did too.